W9-CBY-186

HAMSTER

TO ANDREA–C.L.   FOR BRODY–D.A.

No part of this publication may be reproduced, stored in a retrieval system, or transmitted in any form or by any means, electronic, mechanical, photocopying, recording, or otherwise, without written permission of the publisher. For information regarding permission, write to Scholastic Inc., Attention: Permissions Department, 557 Broadway, New York, NY 10012. • ISBN 978-0-545-49301-7 • Text copyright © 2011 by Cynthia Lord. • Illustrations copyright © 2011 by Derek Anderson. All rights reserved. Published by Scholastic Inc. SCHOLASTIC and associated logos are trademarks and/or registered trademarks of Scholastic Inc.
12 11 10 9 8 7 6 5 4 3 2 1   13 14 15 16 17 18/0 • Printed in the U.S.A.   08 • First Scholastic paperback printing, January 2013 • The display type was set in Coop Black. • The text was set in Cochin Bold, Gill Sans Bold. • The art for this book was done in acrylics. • Book design by Marijka Kostiw

5/18/13

To: Khalil
From: Diamond
&
Jeremiah

HAPPY BIRTHDAY, HAMSTER

HAPPY BIRTHDAY, HAMSTER

By
Cynthia Lord

Pictures by
Derek Anderson

Scholastic Inc.

Best day, bake day, candles on a cake day!
Clap day, cheer day, party time is here day!

Pink cake, blue cake,
chocolate through and through cake.
Short cake, tall cake, cannot eat it all cake.

Which would *you* choose?

Spin toys, glow toys, wind it up and go toys.
Soft toys, hard toys, ride it through the yard toys.

Which would *you* choose?

Games, check. Hats, check. Piñata and some bats, check.
Plates, check. Spoons, check. Streamers and balloons, check.

Which would *you* choose?

Curly fur, straight fur, awesome groovy-great fur.
Striped fur, white fur, looking quite a sight fur.

Which would *you* choose?

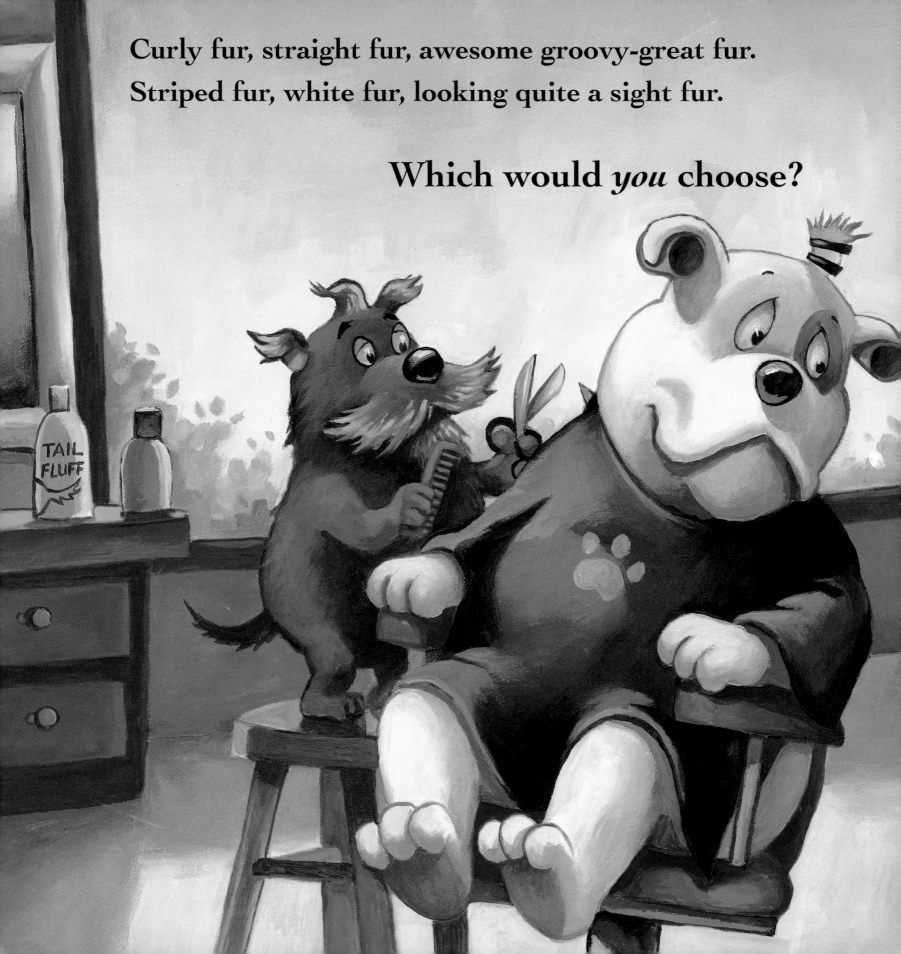

Long day, late day, all I did was wait day.
Frown day, fret day, how could they forget day.

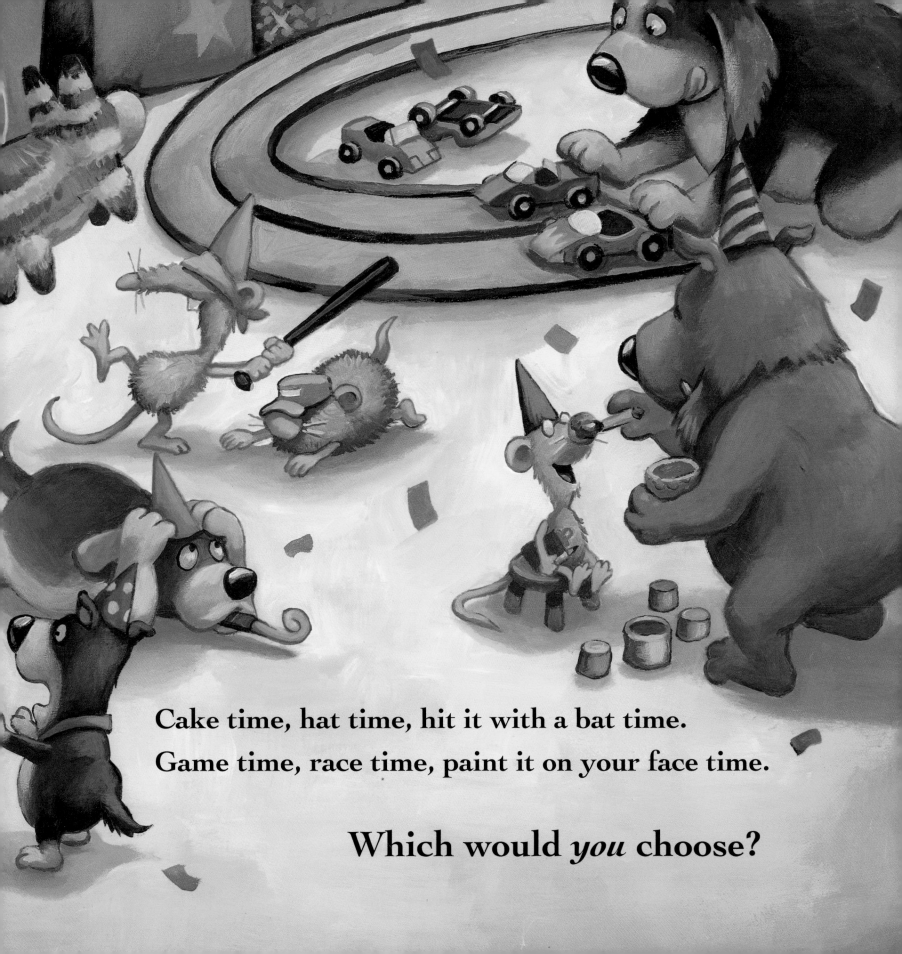

Cake time, hat time, hit it with a bat time.
Game time, race time, paint it on your face time.

Which would *you* choose?

Red box, brown box, sparkles up and down box.
Tall box, wide box, what could be inside box.

Which would _you_ choose?